Sex in Cars

Vol 1

Guy New York

Sex in Cars

Vol 1

by Guy New York
ISBN: 9781730970894

Sex in Cars

Vol 1

Guy New York

The View

"Of course I loved you."

"It doesn't matter," Sarah said, her right hand out the window holding a cigarette.

I drove silently because maybe she was right. Of course, it didn't change the fact that we were in the car together on our way to who knows where just because we bumped into each other at the bar. It had been four months since we broke up and we hadn't seen each other once. Hell, we hadn't even talked since I walked out.

Until now.

"Where are we going?" I asked, turning left onto the dark highway. It was more of a two-lane deathtrap than a real road, but it was so familiar that I didn't even think as I pushed the car up to seventy.

"You're the one who said we should get out of

the bar. And you're the one who keeps trying to look down my shirt."

"I wasn't!" I said, pushing back an embarrassed laugh. What the hell was wrong with me because she looked hotter than she ever had and I was perving so hard it hurt.

"It's nice to know I can till distract you," she said, raising her left foot up and resting it on the dashboard. Her dress slid up her thigh until I could almost glimpse her panties in the dark.

"Don't distract me too much," I said, turning and gawking at her without any shame that time. "I'm not complaining, but if you keep it up, I'm going to have to pull over."

"And what would you do then? Come on, we didn't fuck for like two months before we broke up and it's been forever since then anyway. You don't have the nerve or the inclination."

"How do you know?" I said, trying to sound flirtatious.

"Because I know you," Sarah said, lifting her other leg until her dress fell in between them exposing both thighs. "But you can look all you want."

"Seriously, you're going to get us killed," I said, staring at her legs and wondering how I had never noticed them before. Not like this.

"You're the one driving."

The turnoff wasn't hard to see, and maybe I had been going there without knowing it. Either way, I drove into the small parking lot that looked out over the river and pulled into a spot next to a fogged up Toyota.

What the hell was I doing?

"That's better," I said, turning to face her. Her window was still down, and she lit another cigarette as she pushed her chair back until she was lying nearly flat. The smoke curled around the overhead light, and I wanted to touch her so badly I almost had to get out of the car.

"Those people are fucking," she said, waving a hand at the car next to us.

"That's what people do here."

"I knew you still wanted me. As soon as I saw you at the bar, I knew you missed all of this. Now, look at you. You're eying me like a prized calf, and I bet you're hard."

"I thought you didn't think I had it in me."

"You don't. And besides, we don't have a condom. And if there's one thing I definitely know about you it's that you'll never fuck without one. Even after ten fucking months of me begging. You know, you're a real idiot sometimes? A week after

3

you left me I got fucked the right way again. Christ, it had been so long since I felt an actual dick in me."

"I don't believe you," I said, reaching over and stealing one of her cigarettes. "There's no fucking way."

"You don't have to believe me, Mr. Overly Careful."

"That's a terrible nickname," I said, lighting it as I tried to look up her dress.

The truth was I instantly pictured her doing it with some ex-boyfriend or maybe some other as-shole. She had begged me. For the whole time we were dating she told me to just put it in her, and I said no every time. And suddenly all I could think about was some jerk-off doing what I never did.

"I like you this way," she said, sliding her dress up until her white cotton panties were visible. "Keep on looking at me just like that."

"Like what?" I asked, wondering if I could see the outline of her lips through the fabric. Fuck, did she shave?

"Like you want to fuck me almost as badly as you want to be a good boy. Can't you just fucking stop thinking sometimes? Like for ten minutes?"

"You're so hot," I said throwing my butt out the window and leaning over her. I parted her thighs

4

with my left hand, and she laughed as she stared at me, daring me to do anything. When I slid it up higher, she just opened her legs wider. I stopped before my fingers brushed the elastic and she shook her head as she unbuttoned the top three buttons of her dress.

"You miss it," she said, pulling the fabric open until her breasts reflected moonlight.

"Miss what?" I asked, staring at her like it was the first time. Hell, maybe it was the first time, because if she had looked like this before, then I was a goddamn moron.

"This," she said, waving a hand over her body. "Too bad you're such a nice guy."

"Is that what you think?" I said, moving my hand between her legs until I cupped her pussy over the fabric. I practically climbed on top of her as I leaned in until our mouths were inches apart.

"You'd never," she said, a slight moan escaping with her words. I put more pressure on her, and she sighed again as I pressed my fingers against her. It was apparent in a second that she was utterly smooth beneath the fabric and I cursed her under my breath.

"You're wet," I said, my mouth against her ear. And to prove it I slid my down the front of her underwear until I felt that smooth wet skin I barely remembered. She reached over and began to rub me through my jeans, and it was my turn to moan as her clever fingers traced my cock perfectly.

"You're fucking hard," she whispered. "You want me so badly, but you can't do it. Just say it. Tell me you want me."

I kissed her without warning. Her lips were full and soft, and she tasted like Parliaments and regret, and my entire body craved her like never before. Her breasts beneath my hands were heaven, and as I kissed her neck, I forgot we had broken up. For ten glorious seconds, I felt her body against mine as I touched her, and it was like nothing had happened.

"I want you, Sarah," I moaned, and then I moaned it again, my fingers pushing inside her as I admitted everything.

"I'm right here," she said, pulling my jeans open and taking me in her hand. "What's stopping you?"

"That's not fair," I said, feeling my cock twitch at her familiar touch.

"It's not supposed to be fair; it's supposed to be payback."

And then I did the only thing I could think to do. I climbed over her as I moved down and kissed her between her breasts. Somehow I fit my knees into the space between the seat and the glove box, and I didn't stop. Her dress opened all the way as I kissed down her body until I was met with a tiny pink bow on the front of her underwear.

I slid the cotton off her, somehow managing to move her legs about so I could relieve her of them, and then I opened her thighs, looked up at her smiling face once more and pressed my mouth against her smooth cunt.

"Oh fuck," she moaned, grabbing me by the hair and holding me firmly in place. "You're such a good boy."

She tasted so much like Sarah that I nearly lost myself. Instead, I kept going, shoving fingers inside her as I kissed her thighs, licked her lips and then fucked her with my tongue pretending I could make my way inside her. She clenched her legs around me and arched her back as I did my best, but the truth is I wasn't thinking about much of anything.

I was so caught up in my desire that I did what came naturally. I did what I wanted most in each second, and I didn't stop. Even as she pulled my hair and told me someone was watching I didn't stop. Even when she laughed at me, I kept going. And even when she said I should fuck her instead, I kept going.

It must have been twenty minutes before she managed to pull me up. And even then I kissed her stomach for a long time, my fingers still tracing the smooth skin of her pussy as I marveled at her beauty. But I slowly made my way back up until I kissed her mouth and my god was I still hard!

"It's too bad," she said, biting my ear as she grabbed my ass. I wanted her hand on me, touching me against as I held her, but she didn't let go.

"What is?" I asked, finally rubbing against her in desperation.

"That you can't fuck me. That you have so many dumb rules. That you're missing out on fucking the tightest pussy in the world. Imagine how good I'd feel? Imagine how much better it would be?"

"Fuck!" I yelled as I leaned up, bracing my hands on the seat as we looked down between us. My cock was nestled against her, and it would only have taken a quick push to be done with it.

"You're so close," she said, opening her legs wider. "So close to heaven."

Her laughter was infuriating, and there was no way I was going to let her be right. I wanted her in the worst way, but if I gave in, all those months of restraint would be meaningless. If I gave in now after months of separation and months of fantasizing about doing just that, it would make me even weaker than she claimed I was for stopping.

"Rob didn't hold back," she said, pulling my head down to her once more. With her other hand, she grabbed my cock and began to rub me against her soaking wet skin. "He fucked me so hard. And you know what I like. Just because you never did it, doesn't mean I didn't tell you."

"Don't say it," I begged, trying to stay still. Trying to think clearly. Hell, trying to think at all.

"I love come so fucking much," she moaned, biting my ear before kissing my mouth again. "I love it all over me. On my face, in my mouth, on my tits. I want to rub it into my skin. I want to be covered in it."

"Sarah, stop," I said, feeling her hold me right at her entrance.

"But most of all, more than anything else in the whole world…"

"Don't," I pleaded.

"More than anything, I want it inside me."

"Oh god yes," I said, my shame vanishing behind my desire.

And then, with both of us looking down, I did it. Slowly, almost painfully, I began to push into her, my bare cock feeling her soft skin around me for the first time ever. Hell, my bare cock feeling anyone's skin for the first time ever.

"Are you gonna stop? Are you gonna pull out before you really get to fuck me?"

I kissed her as I felt my eyes tear up. I kissed her, and I filled her at the same time, and for a moment I thought it was love. As I began to move, sliding in and out of her as she laughed and moaned and told me how good it felt, I forget everything.

"It's amazing," I moaned incoherently. "It's... Its'..."

"So much better," she said, grabbing my ass as I fucked her harder and faster.

"Yes," was all I could say, the admission no longer hurting as much as I thought it would. Maybe it was the pleasure of her body that drowned it out or perhaps it was my own acceptance that lessened the sting. But whatever it was I stopped holding back as I fucked my beautiful and terrible ex with everything I had.

"Don't stop," she moaned, somehow wrapping her legs around me. "Don't stop until you come and don't fucking pull out! Don't you dare."

"I don't want to," I said, knowing it was true. "I want to..."

"Admit it," she moaned, clenching around me

10

like she could pull me all the way inside her. "Come on! I know what you want."

"I want to come inside you, what the hell was wrong with me? You feel too good. It's not fair."

"It was never fair," she said, and then we stopped talking. Because then I noticed there were in fact faces peering in the window watching my mistakes. Maybe there was a hand on a cock, and maybe someone's dress was raised up. Through the steamed up glass, I could only see shapes, but it was enough.

I was fucking my ex-girlfriend after more than a year of saying no, and I was going to come. She had me, she knew me, and she won after all that time. And still, I kissed her and cried as I felt myself tense as the end drew near.

And in those last minutes, everything but the feel of her skin vanished away. The car, the people, the smoke, the seats, even her mouth and her breath. All I knew was that I was inside her and it still wasn't enough. Not close enough. Not hard enough. Not long enough.

Not enough to make it last.

I kissed her as I pulled one leg up, my hand hard on her ass. She held me tight as I started to come, and I didn't move as I let myself go within her. And I came, and I came, harder than I had in ages and it didn't matter. Her laughter was sweet instead of taunting and her mouth tasted of forgiveness.

I cried out in the end, the last of me entering her as I tried to pull her closer. She touched my face with a gentle hand. Looking up, I felt it leave me, and then I was back to her, kissing her, again and again, as everything came back in an instant.

It was awkward finally sitting up and pulling out, but faithful to her testimony, Sarah reached between her legs the moment I left her and began to gently touch herself as she looked up at me with a grin. I managed to get my jeans back on, but she lay there exposed and naked in the darkness while the remaining voyeurs looked on with fascination.

Not once did I look away as she made herself come. I didn't touch her, that would have been too much, but I watched her all the same, her sticky fingers pushing inside her as she circled her clit with her other hand all the while whispering the same thing over and over again.

"I knew you wanted me. I fucking knew you wanted me."

Sarah didn't button her dress before she lit another cigarette. She did put the seat up and roll the window down enough to scare off the stragglers. Sweat beaded on her skin as I looked out over the river, and I felt too many things to say any of them. I leaned back in my seat, never looking away.

"You should take me home," she finally said, turning back to me.

The spell was broken in an instant, and the truth hit me all at once. We had broken up and moved on. She belonged to herself, and so did I, and none of that was going to change. After everything we did, it was precisely the same as before.

I put the car into reverse and pulled out just as the cops turned their spotlights on. As I drove down that narrow strip of parking lot, I heard them over the loudspeakers telling the crowd to clear out. The view is closed. Everyone go home.

She kissed me on the cheek when I parked outside her house. I touched her, but she pulled away with a small shake of her head. There might have been a tear on her lash, but possibly it was a trick of the light.

I watched her as she walked up to the house and pulled out her keys.

She never looked back.

The Best Sex Toy Ever

"I just got the best sex toy in the world," she whispered in my ear. "It's outside around the corner."

"Your sex toy is around the corner? What is it?"

"It's my dad's 1966 Buick Electra."

"You're fucking with me!" My mouth was hanging open, and my eyes were wide.

She took me by the hand and pulled me outside, around the corner, down the quiet street until we stopped in front of her little toy, sitting there under a street lamp like it had grown there.

She reached out with the keys, opened the front door and climbed in on her hands and knees. The front seat was so big that by the time she crawled over to the driver's side I was in behind her with a hand up her skirt.

I slid my fingers up the back of her thigh, and I leaned in and kissed her perfect ass. She rolled over and leaned against the door looking at me seductively.

"What do you think?" She asked as she pulled the straps of her dress off her shoulders. With the other hand, she pulled her dress up on one side until

14

she was a pornographic vision of bare breasts and black panties. I leaned in and kissed her, and she undid my tie as I pulled the black silk off her hips. I bumped the steering wheel as I moved my mouth down to her neck and breast, and she tried to get at my zipper around the blinker.

I finally leaned back on the huge bench seat and pulled her to my lap. I tugged both straps down and kissed her ample cleavage as she lifted me hard and ready from my jeans. She teased her lips with the head of my cock, making sure we were both ready, and as she slowly lowered herself down around me she whispered in my ear.

"Daddy would be so proud. It's just like when I was in school."

I pulled her to me and kissed her again. She loves to talk during sex, and there was nothing I could do but enjoy it.

"You fucked in this car in high school?" I asked.

"I lost my virginity right here," she said as she placed her hands on the ceiling. "I was sixteen, and no one would have known a damn thing if Dad hadn't noticed a footprint on the front window."

I rolled her onto her back, so I could fuck her properly, and her foot shot out to just where it must have been all those years ago. Her story moved into

15

pleading, and we grunted and squeaked on the leather seats as our skin struggled for contact. Every once in a while I'd see the lights of a passing car go by, and I'd fucked her harder. I could tell she was coming when she told me to pull her hair, and when she said someone was watching she was long gone. She screamed, and I moaned as I exploded inside her; we bit each other's lips until they were tender and red.

Back at the bar, I asked her how long she had the car.

"Two weeks."

"So, we can do that again?" I asked.

"Next time you have to be driving it."

After The Party

I didn't want to break up the party, but sometimes you have to be an adult. Even when you don't feel like one.

My daughter was eighteen, on her way to college, and apparently capable of taking care of herself. She was also, apparently, capable of throwing a party for seventy-five drunk ex high school students with enough booze to put down an antelope.

So, while I didn't yell, or call the cops for that matter, I did ask the kids to clear out so I could go to sleep before the sun came up. They filed out somewhat quickly, and either stumbled home on foot or hopped into one of the cars with a sober driver.

I checked every one of them.

But then it was two am, Stacy was passed out in her room, and two of her friends were standing on the front step fluttering their eyelashes at me. Okay, it was only Kimmie who fluttered her eyelashes, but her boyfriend Rob smiled and stood up straight and tried to act more mature than he looked.

They were both excellent students. They were friendly, polite, and even funny on occasion. But that didn't mean I was enthralled by the idea of driving their drunk asses home when I just wanted to drink a beer in bed and jerk off.

"Please, Mr. G? I promise we'll be quiet and good."

Now, why the hell would she say that? Kimmie smiled at me though, and if I happened to notice her shirt was unbuttoned halfway down, I didn't say anything about. But I finally agreed because it was better than them sleeping over, and ten minutes later I had two eighteen-year-olds in the back seat of my car as I pulled out onto the quiet and empty streets.

True to her word, they were quiet. In fact, it took me four or five minutes to realize they were making out.

As much as I sighed internally though, I kept my mouth shut because I was in no mood to give a lecture. And what the hell? It wasn't like they were hurting anyone. Or it was my business.

"He's gonna see," I heard a moment later.

Shit, that was just what I needed.

I sat up straight, rubbed my eyes to keep myself awake, and then I peered in the rear view mirror, because why the hell not? Luckily I managed to keep us on the road, in spite of the view, which included Kimmie's shirt all the way open as she leaned over her boyfriend's lap.

I don't know if they saw me, or cared, but he smiled as her head began to bob up and down behind me. Fuck this was not what I agreed to. They were both sweet, but they were far too cute to be doing that shit in the back of my car. And the fact that they were legal didn't make it much better.

Focusing on the road, I found myself adjusting

my growing cock. I could hear little slurps behind me, and maybe the hint of a moan or two. When I thought I could get away with it, I peeked once more to see the bastard pushing her down with both hands, and it was too much.

I turned the corner, sped up as fast as I dared, and then we were there.

The second I stopped the car, I heard the slightest moan before Kimmie reappeared licking her lips. She held her shirt closed with one hand, and when I caught her eye in the mirror, the girl just smiled at me. And winked.

"See you later, Rob!" She said as her boyfriend stumbled out of the car and up the short walk to his house.

I sighed my relief as I pulled back onto the road to take my second charge home.

"I'm coming up," Kimmie said, not giving me a chance to tell her not to. She crawled up between the seats and plopped her cute ass down in the passenger seat before leaning it back and letting out her own sigh.

"Jesus Kimmie," was all I managed to say as her shirt fell open once more.

"Tell me about it. If I suck his dick one more time without getting any, I'm gonna lose my shit.

He's a nice guy, but hello? I have some fucking needs too."

"Do you mind?" I asked, waving a hand at her.

"Oh come on. You just watched me blow that guy, are you really offended by my tits?"

So, I did the only thing I could do. I pulled the car over to the side of the road and put it in park. And then I turned to face her as she did the same to me.

"What is it you think you're gonna get out of this?" I asked as she licked her lips one more time. But while I tried to sound authoritative, the fact that I was staring at her bare breasts probably ruined some of the effect.

"I don't know," she said, looking honestly shy for the first time since I had known her.

"I see," I said, adjusting myself one more time, with less subtlety than the situation probably called for.

"I'm eighteen," she whispered.

"I'm forty," I said.

"I want you so fucking badly," she blurted out.

And before I could think any better of it, I pulled her to me, kissed her on the mouth, and slid my hand up her body to cup one of her perfect tits. She kissed me back, and I grew harder than I had in years. When she reached down and touched me, I had to bite my lip, and when she pulled away just long enough to pull her panties off from under her skirt, I stopped.

I sat up straight as she blushed and leaned back against the window.

"Show me," I said, taking every fucking bit of responsibility. If I was going to do something stupid, I wasn't going to let myself believe it was her damn fault. I wanted her, and I knew better.

And I really didn't care.

Kimmie raised her skirt, and she smiled as she reached between her legs to cover her pussy. The fabric slid up around her waist, but still, I couldn't see a damn thing. Other than her thighs, her stomach, and a hint of what lay underneath.

I took a deep breath as I reached down and released myself from my pants. But since I had already thrown myself under the bus, I didn't bother to hide a damn thing. Instead, I slid my hand up and down my cock as she stared at me with her mouth open.

"Holy shit," she said, pushing two fingers into her wet pussy. "I had no idea."

"About what?" I said, sitting up straighter as my hand moved faster.

"That," she said, reaching out and touching

me. "Fuck."

I watched as she wrapped her hand around me and then I was kissing her again, this time moving down her chin to her neck and then her breasts. The car was big, but it was still an awkward act of acrobatics to get my mouth on her pussy. Luckily I didn't care, and my god was it worth it.

That girl tasted like everything I though pussy should taste like, and I fingered her and sucked on her clit as she moaned Mr. G over and over again. Kimmie started to come in under five minutes, and I only stopped when she physically pulled me up with one hand in my hair.

"Fuck me," she moaned. "Please?"

"Kimmie," I said, looking up at her as I rearranged our bodies. "Listen to me."

"I know," she began, covering her face and mumbling something about a bad idea.

"No listen to me," I said, raising her head up as I opened her legs and crawled between them. My cock was against her wet skin, and we could no longer see through the fogged up windows.

"What it is?" She said, her big eyes opened wide.

"I want you so badly I can hardly stand it. And I'm going to fuck you until you can't walk straight."

Before she could say a damn thing I thrust into that girl and my god was she perfect. Terribly, horribly, immorally perfect.

And I didn't give a fuck.

Instead, I began to slide in and out of her as she moaned and kissed me and told me how much bigger I was than her stupid fucking boyfriend who hadn't gone down on her the entire time they had dated. And then I kept on fucking her in spite of the weird angle of my leg, the cramp in my back, and the nagging realization that I was doing a very fucked up thing.

"Don't stop," she moaned between kisses. "You feel so fucking good. Fuck me, Mr. G."

And that was it. Those stupid words out of her mouth set me off, and less than a minute later I was buried within her as I started to come. Her eyes opened wide, and she broke out into a smile of joyful surprise as I began to fill her pussy. She kissed me with tiny pecks to my lips again and again as I held her hips and thrust into her, and then she leaned her head back, cried out my name one last time and began to clench around my coming cock.

"Fuck yes!" She cried, her second orgasm rolling through as I kept going.

I was done, but it didn't matter because I had

already said yes and my guilt was not her problem. Instead, I fucked her as I felt myself start to go limp and she kept on going until both of us lay sweaty and exhausted in the most uncomfortable position known to man.

I kissed her one last time before I managed to sit up and pull out at the same time.

"You came inside me!" She said, reaching out and grabbing my hand. "Holy shit! It was the hottest thing that's ever happened to me!"

"Jesus, that was good," I said, resisting the temptation to apologize. Christ, she didn't need that either. I could deal with my own shit the next day as I sat in confession with my dick still hard as I tried not to picture it all over again.

"I needed that so badly. I'm so glad I'm going to college next week and don't have to deal with boys anymore."

"Ah yes, all those college men," I said, trying not to sound too condescending.

"You mean professors," she said, patting her skirt down as she began to button up her shirt.

"Cigarette?" I asked, rolling my window down as I got myself together.

"How mature," she said, taking one from my pack even as she stuck her tongue out at me. "But don't tell my mom. She'd shit if she knew I was smoking."

"I won't if you don't," I said, chuckling as I put the car in gear.

We drove in silence through the quiet suburban streets as we smoked out our respective windows. She tucked her knees up just enough that I could still get a good look at her legs, and part of me wanted to bring her home, hide her in my room, and fuck her until she left for school. The other half of me wanted to turn myself in even though I hadn't broken any fucking laws.

"Hey, thanks for the ride, Mr. G," she said, as I pulled up to her house. "And you know…"

I leaned in and kissed her cheek. She turned at the last minute and kissed my mouth again, and for a few moments, we held each other like it was perfectly normal. Kimmie took my hand and slid it under her skirt as we made out like teenagers, and she pressed it to her soaking wet cunt.

"Look what a mess you made?" She said.

And then, before I could think of a witty response, she opened her door, slid out, and slammed it behind her. I watched her go, and for a moment I thought that was it. But then she turned, leaned in through the open window, and kissed me on the lips one last time.

And then she was gone, and I was left alone in a car that smelled like sex and cigarettes and bad choices I wouldn't trade for a million dollars.

I lit another and pulled back onto the street.

It was dark and quiet, and while I might be going to hell, I was going with a smile on my face.

A Smoke, a Fuck, And a Hot Dog

I fucked a mermaid.

I was sitting on the beach by Coney Island with a bottle of Jack Daniels crying about my dead cat when she walked out of the waves. It was February, and the beach was empty as snow fell on the barren shore.

At first, I just saw her head and thought I was seeing things. As she moved closer to the shore, she went from bobbing to walking and before I knew what was happening a perfectly naked woman was walking towards me from the water.

She walked right up to me and asked if she could borrow my coat. I pulled it off my shoulder and wrapped it around her hoping the thick wool would warm her body.

"Do you have a car," she asked. "And a smoke?"

I handed her a Camel as I took her by the hand and walked her over the boardwalk to my 78' Nova. I cranked the engine, turned on the heat and we crawled into the back seat. She lay down on my lap, still smoking her cigarette, and pulled my hand inside the coat to her warm, soft body.

She ran my hand over her breasts and then down between her legs. Her skin was smooth and wet, and she moaned from her throat when I slid two fingers inside of her.

"I only have an hour on land," she told me. "Then I have to return, and this beautiful cunt will disappear beneath my tail. I need a smoke, a good fuck, and a hot dog."

She flicked the cigarette butt out the window and opened my coat in invitation. I fumbled with my pants until my cock was in my hand and I rubbed it against her flesh. She opened her thighs and pushed down towards me until I was inside her. Her mouth and neck and breasts tasted like salt, and she asked me for another smoke.

She lay on her back in the car smoking as I fucked her as best I could. She smelled faintly of fish and seaweed with a hint of sunscreen as an after note. She showed me just what to do, and soon she was screaming and moaning and coming so loudly I thought we would wake up the entire shoreline.

Minutes later she pulled me out of the car behind her, and we ran hand in hand back towards the boardwalk. We found the lone hot dog cart in the cold wind and snow, and I bought her three hot dogs, which she devoured in quick succession.

I followed her back down onto the sand, and she kissed me before handing me my coat. I watched her as she strolled back into the surf until she dove headfirst into the water, and all I could see was the flop of a gloriously red tail before it too disappeared in the white-capped waves.

When I finally returned to my car I heard the soft mew of a cat. I climbed into the driver's side and sitting on the bench seat next to me was the most adorable kitten I had ever seen. Tied around its neck was a note in bubbly letters that simply read "thanks."

Telling Stories

It was two in the morning, and as the cab meandered its way across the island, her stories slipped out. We were four months in, and I felt I knew her well, but there's something different about geography. There's something different about placing everything on a map.

She lived over there with a boyfriend for two years when she first came to New York. She didn't know how he was paying the rent until his roommate went to jail for selling coke to NYU students. It had a view of the park, and they used to fuck in the window on Sunday mornings.

The bar we just passed is where she met her ex-girlfriend. The one who promised not to leave and then left. They flirted all night and spent the next four days together, not leaving each other's side even once. They never want back to the bar, but she remembers it all the same. Eight months of bliss and misunderstanding.

On the other side of town she points out an old office, a coffee shop she worked at years ago, and another bar she got thrown out of for fucking in the bathroom. The pool table had a tear down the middle, and it screwed up her shot every time.

As we get closer to home, I ask her what story she'll tell about this. What will she say years from now when she drives by with someone else to a different apartment altogether?

She leans against me and is quiet for a long time. I kiss her hair, wondering if I've said the wrong thing. I fell in love when I lived here, she whispers, taking my hand in hers. I fell so madly in love I got drunk and told silly stories.

Is that it? I ask, holding her tighter.

That's it, she says, kissing my fingers over and over again. That's it.

Taxi Ride

It was almost 3am, and I was ready to leave. The party was excellent, the crowd was hot, and I was fucking tired.

As I grabbed my coat, a tall, leggy blond walked up to me. She had on this tiny silver dress that clung to her body in all the right places.

"So, um, Michael tells me you live on the upper west side?"

Was that a question? Think quickly. "Um yeah. Why?"

"Well, like, do you want to maybe, share a cab or something?"

I knew what that meant: I'd pay for the cab, and she'd talk about lipstick. If I was lucky though, she might pass out and not talk my ear off the entire way.

"Uh, sure. You ready to go?"

I saw Michael wink at me as we turn towards the door. Thanks, buddy.

She walked towards the curb, and a cab pulled across three lanes of traffic to a screeching halt in front of us. She didn't seem to notice, so I opened the door and climbed in. She was right behind me.

"Um, Broadway and like 76th," she said as she leaned back against the door looking at me. She looked hot. And drunk. And bored. Ce la vie.

I had no idea what to say to this girl as the cab started driving uptown, so I didn't say anything. She looked out the window. Then back at me. Then at the cab driver. Then again at me. She looked me up and down just like I was doing to her, and got a look in her eye.

She leaned forward. "So, like Mr. Cabbie? Do

you mind if I like totally give this guy a blow job?" I wasn't sure if I should laugh or unzip my pants. I did neither.

In a thick Indian accent, I heard him say from the front seat, "I don't mind, as long as you take your top down first."

This must be some sort of NYC agreement I've never heard of before because two seconds later she reached around the back of her neck, untied the straps to her dress and pulled it down to expose two small, perfect breasts.

"They're like kinda small, but I think that's totally in right now. I mean, Paris's are small too, but mine are nicer than hers. You know?"

Suddenly I realized she was talking to me.

"Um, yeah, totally" is what I lamely managed to come out with.

I looked over at her, and before I knew what was happening she leaned over me, opened my jeans, and my god, I was harder than I've ever been. She swallowed me entirely then pulled up and sucked me like a lollypop. My temptation to laugh was gone out the window as one of her hands cupped my balls and the other squeezed tightly around my shaft. Her lips and tongue and everything else were all over me, around me, and doing things I didn't

32

know could be done.

I moaned. Then I moaned again.

"Oh God, Paris," I said just loud enough that I was sure she heard me. I slapped myself in the face.

In my mind.

Just when I thought she was about to kick me out of the car, she sucked harder, took me all the way down her throat while somehow still licking me, and I began to explode. She never stopped as I came and came until finally, she sat up.

She wiped her mouth. She pulled her dress up and tied it in the back.

"Next block on the right side."

Then to me, "Did you, like, totally call me Paris?"

"Um, yeah," I stuttered, looking down into my lap.

She opened the car door and got out. Just as I thought she was gone, she leaned her head in and whispered, "It was totally hot."

Then it was me and the cabbie driving up Broadway.

Driving To Miami

"Guys, if I don't get laid the second we get to the beach, I'm going home."

"You are such a slut!" Marco said, turning to look at the blonde girl in the backseat of the convertible. "We're not even there yet, keep your clam in the bag."

"Oh come on, like you two aren't going to be getting the D all over the fucking place."

"Hey, we are a very nice couple who only do nice couple things," Danny said, reaching a hand over to his boyfriend's knee and giving it a bit of a squeeze. "Of course, now that we took the pill..."

The three friends were just a few hours away from Miami, and already they could feel the pill starting to take effect. At first, it was just a feeling of warmth along with the realization that they no longer had to worry about STI's, but it didn't take long for the side-effects to kick in. Marco and Danny were practically bursting from their shorts in the front seat, and Emily in the back was about to start stripping she was so turned on. Not that she wore much to begin with, but somehow even her bikini top and short pink skirt were starting to feel like too much. Maybe she was a big slut, but wasn't that the point? Not only were they about to hit spring break in Miami Fucking Beach, but they had all taken the damn pill. Shit was going to get crazy.

"I can't believe it's actually happening," Emily said, leaning forward between the two front seats. "You guys aren't really going to stay faithful are you?"

"I don't know," Danny said, turning to face his boyfriend with one eye still on the road. "But I'm about ready to lose my shit. I don't know what is in that pill, but I'm gonna come in my pants if the wind blows any harder."

"Well, I can help with that," Marco said, turning to wink at Emily before leaning over the driver's seat. He undid Danny's shorts with deft fingers, and a grabbed his nearly hard cock in one hand. Sliding his fist up and down, he leaned forward until it was almost in his mouth. Danny had to lift his arms up, and the car swerved to the left as he sped down the highway.

"Fuck, that's hot," Emily said, still watching. "Assuming you don't kill us all."

"He's so goddamn hard. He never gets this hard at home."

"Well, maybe it's because you talk too much!"

Danny said, pushing the other boy's head down. Marco didn't need much more convincing before he started to suck that cock like a pro. With one hand on his shaft and his thick lips wrapped around it, he worked his boyfriend over with well-practiced skill. Danny moaned and pushed his head down, and Emily was surprised they didn't crash instantly. But somehow Danny kept on driving as he received the most epic blow job she had ever seen.

Emily leaned back as she watched, and slid her panties off under her skirt. This was way too much, and besides, if they were going to fuck around, why shouldn't she? She pulled up the pink fabric and spread legs as she leaned back and started to touch herself slowly. With the roof down anyone who drove by could see, but none of them cared. It was fucking Pill Day, and it was perfect.

"Oh fuck, I'm gonna come," Danny said, as his boyfriend took him all the way into his throat. Marco tightened his hand around the base of his cock, came up for air once, and then swallowed him again as Danny started to fill his mouth over and over again. "Holy shit, I can hardly see the road!"

"If you kill us, I'm going to be so angry," Marco said, finally sitting up and wiping his mouth. He looked back at Emily with a grin, and she kept on rubbing her bare pussy as trucks drove by and honked.

"It's so not fair," she whined, moving her fingers more frantically. "I need some dick too."

"Marco will help, won't you? He's been dying to play for the other team."

"Oh right, and you've been so supportive of my little desire to explore that side of my sexuality."

"Hey, if you want to go straight, don't let me stop you. Besides, look at poor Emily back there practically begging for it."

"Practically?" She said, leaning forward. "I am begging for it."

She took Marco's chin in hand and kissed him, tasting the come on his lips and wanting so much more. To her surprise, Marco kissed her back before reaching down to feel her up over the top of her bikini. He didn't know what he was doing, but he sure was enthusiastic about it.

"That's actually kinda hot," Danny said, reaching down and grabbing his dick which was already growing hard again. "Go back there with her. Come on; you know you want to."

Marco didn't need any more encouragement before he undid his seatbelt and climbed into the back. Emily moved to one side and put her left foot up on the seat as she leaned back and opened her legs again.

"You want some of this?" She asked, rubbing her swollen pussy.

Marco unzipped his shorts and pulled out a thick cock that was almost ready to burst. He slid his hand up and down it two or three times, before licking his palm and then coating himself with saliva.

"Oh my god, Marco, why haven't you shown me that before? I would do such horrible things to you if you liked girls."

"Who said I don't?" He asked, leaning over her and kissing her again. In the front, Danny adjusted the rear view mirror so he could watch his boyfriend kiss their best friend while he jerked off.

"Have you ever... You know.... Tried it?" Emily asked, reaching down and wrapping her hand around his cock. He shook his head but moved closer until the tip pressed against her wet lips.

"You're so pretty though, and I've thought about it..."

"Just fuck her!" Danny yelled from the front seat. "Come on; you two are driving me crazy! Do it already."

Marco looked up at the mirror, gave his boyfriend the finger, and then before any of them could say a thing, plunged his cock into Emily's tight body in one quick thrust. She grabbed him by the shoulders, arched her back, and took him in as far as she could, screaming out as he stretched her open. She was wet and ready, but his cock was still big, and the instant shock was overpowering.

"Oh fuck, that feels good," she moaned, pulling him to her. He started to move slowly, fucking her in long strokes as she leaned against the door with her legs in the air. "Fuck, your dick is perfect."

Cars honked, truckers yelled, and people cheered as they drove by, but not one person in the car heard a damn thing.

After just a few minutes, Emily put a hand on his shoulder and whispered in his ear. He pulled out and sat up as she climbed onto his lap with her back to him so she could see Danny's face in the rear view mirror. With one hand, she gripped his cock and guided him back inside her as she leaned back with the wind in her hair. He felt incredible, and she was so close to coming that she didn't care about anything. They were driving, they were free, and they were safe.

"Fuck, I can't believe I'm doing this. Your pussy is so wet and tight. I'm gonna come soon."

"You two are crazy!" Danny screamed, pushing the car up to eighty. His dick was still out, and he was still jerking off as he moved from watching them in the mirror to watching the road in front of him.

"Oh god, yes, I'm gonna come too. Don't pull out, let me feel it," Emily moaned, rubbing her clit frantically as she leaned back, taking Marco's cock so deep inside her it hurt just right. She clenched around him, wanting to feel everything, and then they were both screaming and moaning into the wind as he came inside her over and over again. They kept going, they kept fucking, and they kept screaming, and it was the longest and most intense orgasm either of them had had in a long time.

When Emily finally sat up and moved next to her friend, they saw cars on each side with guys and girls leaning out the window yelling at them. One girl pulled up her top and a dude stuck his cock out the window like a dog in the wind. They lay back on the leather seats, not bothering to cover themselves up as they caught their breaths one more time.

"Dude, you fucked a girl!" Danny said, shooting his load as he cried out. He coated his hand, licked it clean, and then kept on driving like it was the most normal day in the world.

"Dude, you fucked me," Emily said, leaning on her friend's shoulder after kissing his cheek.

Marco leaned back and tilted his head up into the sun. He let out a long sigh as he absentmindedly stroked his cock, still wet from Emily's cunt and his come.

"I fucked my best friend, and it was awesome!" He screamed at the top of his lungs.

"Next stop Miami!" Emily screamed. "And when we get there, I'm going to fuck the first guy I meet, I swear to god!"

Emily pulled off her top and waved it in the air while the three friends sped down the highway, the cars, the trucks, and all of their troubles vanishing further and further behind them with each passing mile.

Where Did He End?

"Why were you so quiet in the cab?" I asked her when we walked in the door.

"He had his hand under my skirt."

"I didn't notice that," I said, and I wondered if

I had drunk too much. "How far under your skirt?"

"At first he just touched my thigh, but then I…"

"What did you do?" I asked, suddenly feeling very much awake.

"I just shifted slightly and opened my thighs. It was only a little, but it was all he needed. He began by touching me over my undies."

"And where did he end?"

"I pulled them aside," she whispered as her head fell against my shoulder. We were sitting on the bed, and I kissed her neck as she continued.

"He seemed surprised, but when he felt how wet I was, he was sure. I squeezed my thighs around his hand, and someone he managed to rub my clit with his thumb as two fingers slid inside me."

"You were completely quiet," I said in amazement. She opened my zipper as we talked and I pulled her onto my lap as she continued.

"He wasn't even looking at me, and I don't know what he was thinking. He responded to every little shift in my body though, and it only took three minutes.

"What took thee minutes?" I asked as I slipped easily inside her. She kissed me as I pulled her close and we were silent for a while as we reveled in the

42

sensation.

"Three minutes for me to come," she said. "I didn't expect it, but before I knew what was happening I was drenching his fingers, and he still wasn't looking at me. He knew just what was happening, and he didn't stop until I pulled his hand away. It was just before he got out of the car."

I lay her down on her back and kissed her for a long time. I was only partially driven by the thought of her coming next to me without so much as a whimper. Mostly I was happy to feel her around me, glad to kiss her, and happy to be home.

Neither one of us came before sleep overtook us, but it didn't seem to matter.

"Next time I'll pay more attention," I said after I turned out the light.

"I think I liked the fact that neither of you was paying attention. You were both mesmerized by the lights outside, and it felt almost like I was alone. I like coming by myself."

"I love you," I whispered.

"I know," she said. When I wrapped my arms around her and kissed the top of her head, she was already asleep.

Her Ex in the Backseat

If I wasn't a jealous person, I'm not sure I would have enjoyed watching her suck his cock in the back seat of the car.

To my credit, he was set up to be difficult. They went out for three months and broke up because, "while the sex was the best ever, we just didn't match up." We had been together for only six months when he visited, but somehow a day at the beach seemed like a good idea. Seven beers also seemed like a good idea, as the did the skinny dipping, and the making out in front of him.

To her credit, she did ask first. Actually, it was more of a pleading, but she did bring it up. I was kissing her on the blanket, and she whispered in my ear, "I need to be fucked."

When I slid my hand between her legs, she added, "by both of you." She wrapped her hand around my cock as she said it, then whispered, "please" in a long drawn out moan.

I'm not sure how we made it back to the car, or how he knew to follow us, but within moments she was lying in the back seat with my cock deep inside her. He took his time climbing in, and his eyes moved up and down our bodies as he knelt beside her.

Without even looking she reached her hand up and pulled his cock into her mouth. She moaned as she tasted him and all I could do was watch. After what felt like minutes she put a hand on my thigh and pulled me into her again as she thrust her hips up against me.

We stayed that way for a long time, with him in her mouth and me in her cunt, until I couldn't take it. I thrust faster and faster into her, kissing her neck and face until I knew I was about to come. I pulled out at the last minute and exploded onto her stomach and breasts.

Without waiting a moment, she turned in the back seat, until her head was in my lap and pulled me down to a kiss. Through my barely open lids, I could see him climb between her legs and slide into her. She moaned, and screamed and bit my lip, and he fucked her for all he worth. I reached a hand down and pressed two fingers against her clit, feeling him moving inside her, and I rubbed her frantically as she screamed louder and louder.

Within minutes she was coming and shaking and screaming in ways I had never seen before. I kissed her again as he collapsed on top of her, and all three of our sweaty bodies trembled against the sticky vinyl of the seats.

Thinking of Cars

I'm thinking back to cars and making out in the dark with that hint of fear always stuck in my throat.

There was a view where we parked even though her dad was on patrol, and I went down on her even though it meant scrunching my body up like a slinky on the floor of the passenger seat. She tasted like olives, and I was so scared I stayed hard for days.

By the river, we could sit without being bothered, but the car fogged up so quickly it didn't matter. Her hand in my pants was the furthest we ever went, but my god did we kiss and wasn't that enough?

Once, on a long ride north, she wore a transparent shirt with no bra and as the truckers slowed down to watch she lifted it for them again and again as I struggled to stick to the road. After an hour of teasing, she pulled me from my jeans and took me into her mouth, her ass in the air as she fingered herself on the dark highway. The cars honked, the air horns sounded, and I came in her mouth for the first time in a year.

But of course, the one moment I can't push away no matter hard I try came months after it ended. The cars all along the cliff's edge were all busy doing the same thing, and the second we stopped, we were on each other, tearing at clothes without taking anything off. I lay her back, her jeans around her ankles, as I found my way between her thighs, my cock entering her like we were made for one another. And even later, with faces peering in the window, we never stopped.

It was over, we were done, and yet for that moment, nothing else mattered. Hell, maybe for the first time in all the time we were together, nothing mattered at all, and we screamed out into the night as tourists surrounded us, watching the young couple fuck through steamed up windows until our bodies convulsed in one final release of too many things.

And now I'm thinking of cars, and her, and of love that was too afraid not to get in its own way. I'm remembering vinyl seats, a few broken promises, and years and years of forgiveness. I'm remembering the cracked window and her voice in my ear telling me not to stop even though she doesn't love me.

Stuck in Traffic

The second she undid her jeans and slid her hand inside of them, the traffic slowed to a near standstill.

"Oh god no," she said, with just a hint of a whine. "I was just starting to have fun."

All around us the cars slowed down, and instead of zipping by us, barely able to get a glimpse of anything at all, it was suddenly apparent that the other drivers might, in fact, notice a girl with a hand in her pants.

"Don't stop," I told her, risking a quick glance in her direction.

"Are you serious? People can see me."

"I know. It's terrible. Whatever will they think?"

"This isn't fair," she said, squirming as she looked out the window. The woman next to us was busy on her phone, but she passed us by in a few moments to be replaced by an old man with his chin to the wheel. He was definitely not going to be distracted by anything we did.

"Why don't you pull them down further," I said, wondering how far she was willing to go. She looked at me, then back out the window, and then back at me once more. And then, with a wiggle, she slid her jeans down just enough that I could clearly see her fingers moving between her legs.

"Anyone can see me," she moaned, closing her eyes for a moment.

"Open your legs wider," I whispered as I reached over and pulled one strap off her shoulder. I tugged at it harder as I watched the road until her left breast was bare. It took every effort I had to keep my eyes on the car in front of me.

"Fuck, this is hot," she said, looking up again as she touched herself faster and harder. Another car moved into the spot next to us, and this time a college kid smiled in our direction and waved at her before pulling ahead. Then it was a couple, both of them pointing before we overtook them once more.

"Do you like that they can see you?" I asked. "Do you like that they know you don't care that they can see you? Does it turn you on?"

"No," she mumbled, avoiding the window as each car drew close.

"Oh fuck."

"What is it?" I asked, turning quickly to see an SUV riding alongside us. The man inside was apparently more interested in watching my girlfriend than he was in following the flow of traffic, and for the first time since we slowed down, there was a car next to us that didn't move.

"What's he doing?" I asked, careful not to rear-end anyone.

"He's just watching and smiling at me. I can't look away."

"Is he hot?" I asked.

"Not really, but he's…"

"What? He's what?"

"He's looking at me like he wants to swallow me. He's grinning, and each time I moan, he laughs at me."

"Pull your panties down," I said, adjusting myself through my pants. Fuck this was stupid and hot and both of us should stop. She whimpered for a moment, but then without looking away from him, she slid the cotton down until he had a completely unobstructed view of my girlfriend's fingers in her cunt.

"Oh god, I think I'm gonna come soon."

"Is he still watching?" I asked, already knowing the answer.

"Yes, but he's not laughing. He's licking his lips, and he looks scarier now. I'm glad I'm in the car…"

"Ask him if he wants to fuck you," I told her, wondering again if she would do it.

"Oh god," she said, pushing two fingers deeper inside her as the entire car began to smell like her. My free hand was on my cock, gently rubbing myself through my thin pants as she started to play with her left nipple, never once looking away.

"Ask," I told her again.

"Do you want to fuck me?" She said, her voice barely a whisper.

"Ask him again. Say it over and over again until you're sure that he can make out the words."

I heard her mumble then, the words slipping from her lips like a mantra, and I came close to crashing a hundred times. But she didn't stop touching herself, and he didn't pull away, and her voice was a silent question that needed an answer.

"He's saying yes over and over again. He's telling me terrible things. He wants me to pull over so he can 'use my little pussy.' He wants us to stop at the next exit so he 'can fuck me while you watch.'"

"Jesus, you can hear him?"

"I can read his lips. And maybe hear him a little. His window is down, but it's so clear, oh god I'm gonna come. He just said he was going to fuck my ass over the hood of the car as you watch from the front seat, oh fuck!"

And then she was clenching around her fingers

and moaning as she arched her back and closed her eyes. I could see her in my peripheral vision shaking and smiling as she came, and for a second I saw his predatory look through the open window of his SUV.

Just as she began to come down, and just as I nearly burst from my jeans, the traffic started to open up. She looked up once more and smiled, and then he was gone, speeding in front of us before cutting over to the right lane, passing back to the left, and then vanishing into the once again moving string of cars.

She pulled her shirt up and then her pants as well, and the fading light out the window finally started to obscure us both. I reached out and touched her knee as she settled back into her seat with a sigh.

"Fuck that was creepy," she said. "Creepy and hot. I can't believe we did that."

"I'm just glad he didn't follow us. But yeah, that was amazing. You did such a good job."

"I'm blushing so fucking hard. I feel filthy."

"In a good way?"

She leaned over and kissed me on the shoulder as her hand slid down to my hard cock. Her touch was gentle as she traced my length with one fingernail.

"In the best way," she said.

A Blowjob, a Virgin, And a Car Ride

I'd be lying if I said I didn't have a crush on Katie. Of course, I had a crush on pretty much every girl in school, so maybe it didn't mean much, but she was different. Okay, I never asked her out and I probably would have been a shitty boyfriend, but I wanted her more than I cared to say. I think she knew it too, but while she sometimes made out with me if she got super stoned, it was always a guessing game.

Which is to say that as we drove down that winding road on our way to the Bradfords' I was trying not to pay too much attention to her smoking out the window. She was wearing the tiniest shorts I had seen all summer, and her tank top was loose enough that I could tell she wasn't wearing a bra. To make matters worse, her nipples were hard.

"Does this help?" She asked, pulling her shirt down on one side, so her left tit was sticking out. Her tongue followed.

"Oh fuck you, I wasn't looking," I said as she covered herself again.

"You were staring so hard you almost crashed the car."

"It's not my fault you have great tits."

"It's not mine either. Now pay attention to the fucking road before you kill us."

I laughed as we pulled into the driveway and she chucked her butt out the window. The second the car stopped, she was out the door, and holy shit, that girl's ass kept me up at night. I leaned forward and watched her walk towards the house, and her shorts were a gift from God. Her two perfect ass cheeks were cleft in half by that tight denim, and it was good. Perfect even.

Two seconds later I was behind her as she walked into the house, opened the fridge and grabbed a beer. The Bradfords were never home. At least their parents weren't, which meant that their house was like a youth center for over-privileged white kids. And the rest of us who managed to sneak our way in.

I lost her within minutes, but I knew where she went. I don't know if she had a crush on C, but I do know that she liked to make out with him more often than she did me, and that afternoon something in the air felt different.

But while there were a few other kids hanging

around playing video games, I wound my way up the back stairs, down the second-floor hall, over to the tower, and up into Jenny's room. She was a year older than me and two years older than her brother C, and she was sweet and quiet and pretty as a daffodil. She also wore sweaters that gave me a fetish for tight cotton over perfect breasts.

And she had a boyfriend.

Who happened not to be there.

But when I sat down on her bed and she looked up from reading in the window seat, her smile held a hint of something interesting. So in the full cockiness of youth, I walked over to her, kissed her on the cheek, and then sat down across from her and lifted her feet onto my lap.

"Hello, beautiful," I said.

"You're ridiculous," she said, shaking her head.

"You love me."

"I wouldn't go that far."

"How far would you go?"

Jenny opened her legs and moved in closer until we were practically in each other's laps as we sat facing one another. She wrapped her arms around my neck, leaned down until her forehead touched mine, and then she sighed. It was not a tired sigh or a fed up with your shit sigh. It was a sigh that made my cock twitch as I slid my hands up her back to discover she wasn't wearing a bra under that tight sweater.

"That depends," she whispered. "Brad is coming over later, and I want to give him a present. I thought maybe you could help?"

I had no idea what she was getting at, but I liked all of it. Just as I was about to say something, we heard a yell and a splash from outside. We turned to look out the window only to see her brother and Katie in the pool. She was decidedly topless, and we watched in silence as they teased each other and made waves. When he held her close I felt my stomach tighten, but then Jenny turned my head back to her with a hand on my chin, and she blushed so brightly I nearly came in my pants.

"I want to give him a blow job," she said. I pulled her in closer until our thighs piled together and our mouths were inches away. If I lifted her onto my lap, she would know exactly how I felt.

"I'm listening," I said.

"But I want to practice first."

"So you do it right?"

"Exactly. I want to make sure I'm good at it. I want him to be happy."

"I can help with that," I whispered.

If she wanted a lesson in cocksucking I was perfectly willing to help out, and if it made her silly boyfriend happy later, then who was I to complain? And besides, Jenny's lips were trembling, and I wanted them.

"Let's go to bed," she said, somehow untangling herself and taking my hand. I followed right behind her until I fell on top of her, my hands on her sides just barely brushing the curves of her breasts.

"It's just a blowjob," she said, her lips perilously close to mine.

"Can I kiss you?" I asked, touching her gently.

She turned and let me find her cheek instead as she shook her head. I leaned in and kissed her neck, and she moaned and held me there, my lips against her skin as one knee slid between her legs. She tightened her thighs around it even as she reached down and began to run her hand up the length of my now fully hard cock.

She didn't stop me when I slid one hand under her shirt and finally felt those glorious tits I had dreamt about. But she turned her head each time I tried to kiss her, and she laughed off my attempts to undo her jeans.

I was desperate for her in ways I didn't understand, but I tried to hold back. I could feel the heat between her legs as I rubbed my hand along her thigh before pressing my forearm against her denim-covered pussy. She groaned as I took her in the crook of my arm, pressing into her as I pulled her sweater down just enough for me to find cleavage.

And then she had my jeans open, and she moved down the bed as she rolled me onto my back.

"I just want to practice," she said, looking up at me as she slowly pulled my aching cock from my pants. "It's nothing serious. Tell me how to do it."

"Fuck," I moaned, feeling her open her mouth around me. Her room was a blur as I held her head gently, moving deeper into her as softly as I could. Her touch was tentative and shy, but when she looked up at me, there was an eagerness in her eyes that spoke of playfulness and desire.

I could hear splashing outside in between yells and long periods of silence, and for a brief second, I wondered how far Kaitie would go. Were they doing the same thing in the warm waters of the hot tub?

When Jenny gagged for the first time, I reached down and took her hand in mine, wrapping it around my cock. I showed her how to slide it up and down gently as she took the head between her lips and swirled her tongue around me.

"That feels so fucking good," I said as she began to stroke me faster and kiss me with more and more vigor. "Take it into your mouth again. Not too much, just until you think you might choke and then stop."

She blushed again as she looked up at me, her hand moving faster, and then she was back on me. This time she took my entire length down her throat, and I cried out as I felt myself enveloped in her warm, wet mouth.

The rest is a blur of her hands and lips and what little instruction I gave her was irrelevant. She wanted to suck my cock, and her enthusiasm was infectious. I struggled not to fuck her mouth harder, but the truth was it didn't matter. In less than five minutes she worked me into a frenzy, and I could tell I was close.

"I'm gonna come," I whispered, pulling her head up so I could see her face once more. "You can do it with your hand, or keep going. But it's going to get messy."

"I want to swallow it," she said, and then she was back on me, and there was nothing I could do. I moaned out her name as she worked faster, taking more and more of me each time until I grabbed one of her hands and squeezed as I started to let go.

"Oh fuck!" I cried as she held me in my mouth,

59

swallowing my come with eager joy. She looked up at me the whole time, and her brown eyes were so damn pretty I wanted everything else, too. As I slowed down, she licked me up and down from the base of my cock all the way up to the head, taking every drop of come she could find.

And then she sat back on her heels and smiled while she wiped her mouth. I reached down and zipped my pants up as I tried to catch my breath.

"So? Did I do it okay?"

"Brad is going to be a very happy boy," I said, moving closer to her again. I had just come, but it didn't matter. My brain was a cloud of hormones, and I couldn't help myself. "But let me do it to you, too."

"What?" She asked, licking her lips one more time. "What do you mean?"

"I mean let me go down on you. I want to taste your pussy. I want to see if I can make you come as well. I promise I'll do whatever you say."

"No way," she said shaking her head. "I just wanted to learn that thing."

"Fuck, are you sure?" I asked, picturing it all at once. I wanted her jeans off and her breasts heaving as I climbed between those thighs and tasted her. I had gone down on precisely one girl in my life, and she had been less receptive. Nervous and shy, she told me it was gross and why would I want to do that and all I could think of was how badly I wanted never to stop.

But Jenny shook her head and got up from the bed. She pulled her sweater down and moved back to the window seat. She took a sip from a cold cup of tea and smiled at me like I had somehow done her a favor instead of the other way around.

"That was amazing," I said, unsure of what else to say.

"You better go check on Katie," she said. "Make sure my brother isn't being a fucking asshole or something. I'll let you know what Brad says."

"I expect a full report," I said, finally getting up and leaning against the door. I couldn't take my eyes off her, and I had never wanted to eat anyone's pussy as badly as I did hers. "Are you sure I can't...you know. I can't go down on you? I want to so badly."

"No!" She said, still playful, but this time completely clear. "Now get out of here. Brad will be here soon."

"Okay," I said, shaking my head and opening the door.

"Oh, and thanks again. I think it helped. I feel much better about tonight."

"Glad I could be here for you," I said with a wink I hoped was charming.

And then I was downstairs wondering where Katie and C were, but not wanting to walk in on anything. There was noise from the library, so I went in there to find three friends watching Airplane on the giant TV. Someone offered me a beer which I took and opened, and before I knew it, I was slouched down on the leather couch watching a dumb movie and dreaming of eating pussy.

Katie finally came in an hour later, but C was nowhere to be seen. I got up and went over to her, and she couldn't stop smiling. She wouldn't say a thing, but she was giddy and silly and kept quoting the movie along with everyone else.

When I heard a car door and looked out the window to see Brad arriving, I asked Katie if she wanted to head out and maybe hit up the diner. She nodded, and so we said our goodbyes and headed out the back to my old, beat-up Oldsmobile. Katie handed me a cigarette as I pulled out of the driveway, and I instantly turned right up to the quiet scenic road instead of the main streets infested with traffic lights.

We smoked out the window as Jefferson Airplane blasted out of the old tape deck, and Katie snuggled up next to me on the big bench seat as we drove. Just before the turnoff back into town, I pulled off the road to the overlook. There were a few other fogged up cars parked by the view, but it was a pretty quiet night.

"Jenny sucked my cock," I said.

"No wonder you wanted to leave when Brad got there. Was it any good?"

"Yeah, she said she wanted to practice. But then she wouldn't let me eat her pussy, and now I can't think of anything else."

"I lost my virginity," she said, turning to face me. She lifted her knees up to her chest, and I couldn't read her expression.

"In the pool?"

"Yeah, I was hanging onto the diving board, and C came up and grabbed me. We had been kissing on and off, but as I held onto the board he wrapped his arms around me; he was so fucking hard."

"Jesus, how did that even work?" I asked, my gaze running up her thigh to the small gap between the denim and her leg. It was instantly clear that her shorts now covered nothing but bare skin.

"I don't know. I was hanging on, and somehow he moved my bottoms to one side. And then he just pulled me to him, grabbed onto me with one arm and his thing with the other, and that was it. He was in me, and we were fucking and kissing."

"Damn Katie, that's intense. Was it fun?"

I couldn't look away now as I realized what had just happened and I felt like the biggest pervert and freak in the world. But I knew that just a few feet away from me was Katie's pussy. And she had just had sex. And that was the hottest thing I had ever heard, and I couldn't help myself.

"It was awesome. It didn't last that long, but he felt amazing, and I wrapped my legs around him until…"

"Until what?" I asked, sliding towards her on the big front seat. I pulled one long leg to me as she shook her head and covered her face with her hands.

"Until he finished. You know. Until he came in me."

"Fuck, that's so damn hot," I said. "It's not fair, I've been thinking about pussy all day and now this too. I saw you out the window, but not that part."

"Whatever, you got your dick sucked, what are you complaining about?"

"Pussy!" I said, leaning back as I looked at her tiny shorts. "And right now I'm thinking about your pussy. Show me."

"What? Jesus, that's fucked up."

"Come on. I want to see it."

"You only want to see it?" She teased, reaching down and tugging on her shorts until I had a glimpse of the smooth skin beneath it. "Is that all?"

And then she pushed the damn shorts to the side and there it was. Katie's pussy was right in front of me, and I couldn't look away. It was dark in the car, but it didn't matter. I could see her and smell her, and I wanted her in a million ways.

"That's so hot," I said again as I leaned forward until I had one of her legs in my arms. I kissed her knee and then her thigh as she laughed and leaned back.

"You want a closer look?" She asked.

One time months earlier, I had fingered her under the table at the diner, but this was something else. We kissed on occasion, but now it all felt different. She was my friend, and I loved her, but I wanted to eat her pussy more than anything in the entire world. Even after her sloppy sex in the pool.

"Yes," I said, as I moved higher up her thigh until I was so close she could feel my breath on her skin. When I reached up and undid the button on her shorts, she just laughed, and when I pulled the zipper down, she slapped me on the head. But when

I started to slide her shorts down over that perfect ass, she grew silent as she lifted herself up enough for me to pull them off.

And then Katie leaned all the way back and opened her legs. She looked at me as she slid a hand down and opened her pussy gently with two fingers. I managed to move down onto the floor in front of her as I turned her to me.

"Let me taste you," I said, kissing her thigh again as I forced her legs open wider. "Please?"

"I'm not going to stop you," she whispered. "It might be messy though. C came a whole lot, and he didn't pull out."

"Fuck," I said, wondering if I was messed in the head. But it didn't matter, because Katie's pussy was right there and after wanting Jenny's so badly and being denied, there was no way I could stop. And the fact that Katie had just shaved everything off the night before didn't hurt either.

She was wet and swollen as I slid my thumb up along the right side of her lips before I dove in. I kissed her thighs again as I moved closer, and then I had her. All at once I buried my mouth against her and pushed my tongue as far into her as it could go. She grabbed my hair and screamed, and there was no stopping me. I have never devoured a girl the way I did her, and I wanted to drown.

Somewhere in the middle, I knew I was tasting his come as well, but I didn't care. She was beautiful and wet, and she tasted better than anything had ever tasted. I licked her and fucked her with my fingers, and she moaned and sighed as she pushed me down harder until my tongue pushed against her clit as she held me.

"Oh fuck! That feels so good," she moaned. "He fucked me so hard and now you're kissing me and my god this is the best thing ever."

In less than ten minutes Katie started to come, and still, I didn't stop. My cock was painfully hard in my jeans, but it didn't matter. I licked her up and down in between fucking her with my tongue, and I knew nothing else. She was sweet and salty but most of all she tasted like pussy, and I loved every inch of her. As she clenched around my fingers and pulled my hair, I stayed there, letting her drench my face as she came.

It was only after she began to come down that she lifted me off of her and pushed me away,

"Fuck," she said over and over again, and I looked up at her with a smile. I kissed her leg and her knee and then her thigh again but I didn't go back. She held me at bay with one hand as she touched my face gently until both of us started laughing.

"You're insane," she said.

"You're the slut who got fucked in the pool."

"You're the asshole that got a blowjob from a girl with a boyfriend."

"I think I'm in love with your pussy."

"She only likes you as a friend."

"She's gonna break my heart."

"I want cheese fries. And coffee. And maybe a strawberry milkshake."

"Shit," I said, finally climbing back up onto the bench seat. "Give me another cigarette?"

She handed me one as we rolled the windows down, and it was only then that I realized another couple had been standing right outside the car watching the whole damn thing. They scattered as we blew smoke out the window, but Katie and I began laughing again, and the entire situation was ridiculous. I had just gone down on my best friend. She had just lost her virginity. I had just gotten the best blowjob of my life.

"I need a fucking cheeseburger," I said. "With onion rings on it. And bacon. And maybe a fried egg."

"Let's go," she said, finally getting her shorts buttoned up again. "I'm fucking starving, and I want my first post-virginity disco fries."

I slid the car into drive and chucked my cigarette butt out the window. Katie pulled her legs up again as she slid closer to me on the seat. I wrapped one arm around her as I turned the giant car around and headed back out onto the dark road at the top of the cliffs.

We were silent as we drove to the diner, but the radio made up for everything. I squeezed her hand at the red lights.

She kissed me on the cheek when we parked.

And then it was neon lights, overflowing ashtrays, and our favorite waitress with a cigarette hanging from her mouth and an eternal cup of coffee in her hand.

It was summer, and we were young.

And nothing would ever be that good again.

The Stolen Car

We shouldn't have been fucking in that car.

Maybe we shouldn't have been fucking at all, but it was two am, we had been teasing each other for months, and her boyfriend had recently told her to go out and get laid if she wanted to.

But here are three problems with car sex:

1. It always involves some level of acrobatics to find a position slightly close to comfortable.
2. It's impossible not to start singing Paradise By the Dashboard Light in your head.
3. There's always the possibility that the car will move.

Which brings us back to the story.

It was two in the morning. Her legs were over her head in the passenger seat as I move from tasting her to fucking her. We were parked on a quiet street and humming something about going all the way tonight. The quiet street was also on a hill.

Through some glorious and terrible act of kismet, I managed to thrust into her at precisely the same time my knee managed to knock the car out of gear. But since the first was far more apparent to both of us than the later, it took us until we she was asking me if I would love her forever before we noticed that we were moving.

Now, fucking in a moving car is fun. I've had plenty of great nights with an old friend driving while me and his old lady got it on in the back seat. It can be very liberating.

But fucking in a moving car while nobody is driving is more complicated. Especially when the hill ends not with a soft mound of dirt, not with a line of water-filled orange barrels, and not with a gentle upslope which might eventually let us roll back and forth in our beautiful valley while we finally fucked after too long of wanting.

No, at the bottom of the hill was instead (in this order), a fence, a stream, a manicured lawn, a flower garden, a smaller fence, the side of a house.

It was the first fence that gave us pause. In fact, I nearly pulled out we were so surprised.

The stream we forded easily as she wrapped her legs around me and bit my neck and the manicured lawn slowed us down enough that we considered not worrying at all. The flower garden made a sound that was concerning, but not enough for me to let go of her throat as we fucked harder, and we quickly found ourselves too close to the end to stop for something like flowers.

The smaller fence dislodged us at the exact moment I started to come, but it wasn't until we hit the house that she bounced off the seat, back onto my cock, and began to squirt as she yelled something about a hurricane.

The sudden infusion of light did encourage us to pull up our jeans, and the screaming might have quickened our frantic search for the rest of our things. The sirens tore the song right out of our heads, but it wasn't until we heard the shotgun blast that we dove out the driver's side door.

We made it over the fence with no problem. It was small.

The flower garden had been pretty once, but now it was mostly a mud garden. The lawn was far bigger than we remembered on the way down, and the stream was cold and wide. And if we hadn't smashed through the fence just moments before, we probably wouldn't have gotten over it.

But there, running up the hill where the car had previously been parked, arm in arm, our shirts covered in come and our hair a mess, we decided that there was, in fact, nothing we wouldn't do for love.

Except, maybe that.

A Town We Didn't Know

We picked her up driving through a thunder-storm in a town we didn't know.

We cranked the heat up in the car, and you slipped over the old bench seat with a dry sweater in hand. She peeled off her soaking jacket and shirt without any pause at all, and I watched in the rear view mirror as you helped her pull the sweater down over her goose bump skin. Whispering in the dark you were friends in an instant, your hands warming her own in minutes.

I turned the radio on to find Vin Scelsa's voice murmuring in the darkness. It was matched only by the rain on the hood of the car as I made my way slowly down the dark, winding, country road. Laughter broke through the patterns of sound with giggles and more whispers. She clung to you for comfort, and when I first heard you sigh, I wondered if it was the next song.

Watching through the mirror, she slid her hands inside your jeans, her mouth never leaving your ear. Your legs parted, your lips did the same, and she turned to face you, the muscles in her arm leaping out as she moved with strength and deter-

73

mination. I watched in awe as she grew bolder with each moan that left your mouth, and when she pulled your jeans down to your knees, you smiled at me in the mirror.

On the side of the road, in a rainstorm, in a town we didn't know, I watched you kiss her. On the side of the road in a town we didn't know with the rain falling, I watched your fingers move from thighs to mouths without pausing in between. In a town we didn't know, pulled over on the side of the road, I held your hand as a strange girl opened her mouth between your legs while the rain pounded on the roof of your father's car.

As the rain fell, three warm bodies wrapped each other in a blanket of fleeting connection. On the side of the road, three people drifted in and out of sleep. In a town no one knew, I kissed your hair as a strange girl cried quietly in your arms.

Don't Fuck
My Girlfriend!

"You should come back here and fuck me while we're stuck in traffic. It's not like Jay could do anything about it."

"Hey, I'm right here!" Her boyfriend said, slamming on the breaks for the seventy-sixth time.

"I don't know man, she's looking super cute these days," I said, looking at the girl in the backseat. She was leaning back with her legs open, and her dress was so short I could see her white cotton panties beneath it.

"Shut your damn legs, you slut!" Jay yelled, but Sarah just stuck out her tongue at him and opened them wider.

"Come on, I'm serious. There's no way he could get off the highway in time to stop you. Just climb back, pull it out, and stick it in me."

"You have such a way with words, baby," Jay said, shaking his head.

I looked back and forth between them, because the truth was, I didn't understand their fucking relationship one bit. Every time Jay got drunk he told me I should bang her, and she teased me about it to no end when she was sober.

Even in front of him.

"You guys are crazy," I said, looking back once more. Sarah winked at me, and then when Jay was looking ahead at the road, she pulled her panties to one side and showed me her pussy.

"I'm in," I said, unbuckling my seatbelt. "You're in trouble now, Sarah!"

"Dude, what are you doing?" Jay yelled as I slid in between the seats to the back. I pulled myself up next to his girlfriend, and she started kissing me instantly.

"You know he's told me to fuck you like seven times," I said, trying to pull a leg up so I could grab her ass.

"Only when I'm drunk! I swear baby, I would never."

"Good enough for me!" Sarah said, giving him one last look in the rear view mirror before tearing my pants open and pulling my cock out. She managed to slide to the floor as she took me in her hand and then instantly down her throat.

"Fuck!" I cried out as I looked up at my friend driving the car.

"Is she blowing you? Are you serious? She's

76

sucking your dick while I'm driving the damn car? What the hell Sarah?"

"It's so good," she moaned, holding one hand up and raising her middle finger at him. "I want it in me."

"Fuck you're good at that," I said, leaning forward and pushing her dress down until I could get at her tits. "And you look so hot like that. How have I never seen you topless before?"

"That's actually a good question," Jay said, adjusting the rear view mirror. "She pulls those things out all the time. But seriously Sarah, can you stop blowing my best friend? This traffic is fucking killing me."

"Sure thing," Sarah said, wiping her mouth with the back of her hand before climbing up onto my lap. "No more blowjobs."

I buried my face between her breasts as she grabbed me in one hand and started rubbing me against her soaking wet pussy lips. Jay started yelling something, but Sarah was telling me how bad she wanted it and I couldn't hear anything else.

"Did he really tell you to fuck me?" She asked, loud enough for him to hear.

"At least six times," I said.

"Thanks, baby!" She said, turning her head and

blowing him a kiss as she sank down onto my cock, letting me fill her in an instant.

"Fuck!" I cried, and he started saying the same thing as he tried to pull over through the heavy traffic.

"Are you fucking him? Are you really fucking him, you crazy cunt? What the hell?"

"He feels so good," Sarah said, giving him the finger one more time. "I'm so glad you told us to do this! It was such a good idea, Jay. Did you know he had a bigger cock than you? You must have. Fuck, it feels good, I think I might come."

"Cut it out!" Jay yelled as I grabbed her ass and pulled her to me, kissing her mouth as I frantically thrust up into her. She held me tightly and kissed me back, and each time the car lurched forward she bounced up and down letting me bottom out within her.

"Yeah, slam on the breaks again baby. He's gonna bruise the shit out of me! Do it! Come on!"

"Shit, shit, shit," Jay said, the rear view mirror completely turned so he could watch, and I swear I saw him adjusting his pants with his left hand as he steered with his knee.

"She's so tight, Jay," I moaned, leaning around her and giving him a thumbs up. "Christ, she feels good. I'm gonna nut in her. So fucking hard!"

"Do it, big boy," she moaned, "give it to me!"

"Are you serious? I can't even fucking see anything. Are you two actually banging? For real? Shit shit shit."

"Don't crash baby," Sarah yelled, clenching around me as I kissed her tits one more time, trying to hold back.

"Don't come in her!" Jay yelled.

"That's not what you said last night!" I called back, feeling myself reach the point of no return.

"I was fucking joking!" Jay screamed, finally managing to pull the car off onto the shoulder of the highway. He slammed on the breaks, and I slid forward, my cock pounding into Sarah with all the force of a quick stop.

"Yes!" She cried out as I kissed her again, trying to fuck her harder.

"You fucking slut," Jay said, his seatbelt lost as he quickly turned around. He knelt between the front seats and pulled Sarah's head back so he could kiss her and feel her up at the same time.

"I'm coming!" I yelled, pulling her onto me as I started to let go. She kissed her boyfriend as I flooded her, and he grabbed her by the throat as she grabbed my arms and pulled herself down until her clit pressed against my pelvic bone.

"Fuck, I'm coming too!" Sarah cried, and I swear I could feel it. Jay kept on kissing her, one hand now on her clit as I kept thrusting, and the other still around her neck.

"You two are the worst!" He cried, as our screams filled the car. I bit my lip as the last of my come shot into her, and she clenched and moaned as she struggled for breath. With both hands on her ass, I pulled her forward and buried my face between her breasts one last time before collapsing back onto the seat with my dick still inside her.

"Holy shit, that was hot," I said.

"I'm still coming," Sarah said, shivering as she leaned forward, escaping Jays grasping hands. He kissed the top of her head as she let out one final sigh, and then she started laughing as she turned to kiss him again.

"That was so fucking hot," she said, in between sloppy kisses.

"I hate you both," Jay said. "I didn't even get to come. This is bullshit."

"I can drive for a bit," I said, feeling generous for some reason.

"Fuck yeah," Jay said, sliding over the console and into the back where he grabbed his girlfriend and

80

began kissing her as his hands roamed up her back.

I got out of the car and walked around front. The traffic had somehow lightened while we were parked, and so I buckled up and rolled the window down. I turned up the radio, checked my side mirrors, and then looked in the rear view to see Jay finger his girlfriend as she jerked him off.

"You're in so much trouble," he growled as I pulled back onto the highway.

"You fucking loved it," Sarah said. "Now fuck me before we get to my parent's house. This weekend is going to be so weird."

The Big Black Buick

The car made me want a fucking cigarette. And a seventeen-year-old girl on my lap as we parked somewhere too public to fuck when I was too young to know better.

So, I stopped on the corner and convinced the guy at the bodega to sell me a loosie even though he said they didn't do that. Maybe it was my smile.

Probably not.

I never had a car like, but it didn't matter. The damn bench seat was what did it, and I was stuck down a rabbit hole of suburban teenage fantasies mixed in with enough memory to take me away.

J and I on the highway as she pulls her shirt up and sucks my cock while the truckers pull their horns.

M leaning back on the seat as I kneel on the floor, wedged between the center console and the glove box as I eat her pussy and try to forget her uncle is on patrol that night.

S and I fucking in the front seat with the windows fogged up as someone peers in at us with his dick in his hand frothing at the mouth.

I take another drag and laugh at myself for going back so easily, but there's nothing to be done about it. I haven't driven in months, and the last time I owned a car, it was a practical one.

Practical for everything but sex.

But I said a little prayer for my lost sense of daring and fearlessness. I gave thanks for my muddled teenage brain which wanted to unsnap R's jeans more than it wanted a million dollars. And I offered a eulogy for my desperation, perspiration, ejaculation, flirtation, temptation and elation days of old.

82

I crushed out my cigarette.

And just before I left, I leaned down and patted that car on the ass like it was the most inappropriate fucking thing in the whole damn world.

The Rest Stop

I parked in the shade, and together Lisa and I walked into the rest stop to use the respective facilities. She bought a diet coke and I got a bottle of water, and less than ten minutes later we were back in the car. I filled it up with gas since we hadn't been able to stop the night before, but just as I was about to pull out, she pointed to an empty spot ahead of us by the dog park.

"What is it?" I asked, raising an eyebrow.

"Just pull up next to that pickup truck for a moment," she said, flashing me a big grin. I was skeptical but still curious, so, of course, I did just as she said. If she had half as much nerve as I hoped, we were in trouble. Glorious and beautiful trouble.

"He was watching me on the highway," she whispered, looking back at me. A minute later, a tall white guy in a baseball hat climbed up into the cab and rolled down the window. Just as he was about to pull out, Lisa smiled and waved, and suddenly he wasn't in such a hurry to leave. Her shorts were impossibly tiny, and her tank top had slid down off her bare shoulders.

Like it was the most natural thing in the world, Lisa slipped the straps even lower as the guy in the truck leered at her with no apparent reservations at all.

"Is that all you gonna show me, pretty girl?" He asked quietly. She looked up and shook her head, pulling them all the way down until her small breasts were completely exposed. This was definitely more like it, I thought to myself. Slipping down lower in the seat, she slid her shorts down until they were nearly off her hips completely. Any lower and he'd have almost as good a view as I had just gotten.

"Holy shit girl, you are something. You like showing off, huh?"

"Yeah mister, you like watching?" She said, her hand sliding up and down her body. I was hard in a second, but I was also patient. As turned on as I was, I mostly wanted to know how far she would go. Was my old friend's girl really just a tease, or was there more to her? And how far could I push her?

84

"Show me that little pussy. Come on, you know you want to. I know sluts like you."

"Do it," I commanded quietly, watching her intently. "Show him just how right he is."

"Oh fuck," she said, sliding one hand inside her shorts. From where I was sitting I could see her push two fingers inside herself as he watched from above. She circled her clit, pushing the shorts down even further until he could watch her hand even though it covered her smooth pussy.

"You are so fucking hot," he said, reaching behind him and opening the back door to the truck, blocking the view between the two cars. He opened his door and turned to face her, his hard cock now in hand as he watched her touch herself.

"Jesus," she said, looking over at me for just a moment as this stranger jerked off in front of her. She finally pushed her shorts down even further, letting him see all of her little body, and he moaned out in appreciation, his hand moving faster as he stood up, his cock practically bursting through the open window. From the parking lot, all you could see were his legs, the back door making a decent shield, but still my heart beat in my chest, certain we would be caught at any moment.

"Show me you're not just a tease," I whispered

as he approached her. "Show me you're not just some silly girl playing a game."

"You are such a fucking slut," the guy said again, this time leaning forward as she reached a hand up to touch him. She turned to look at me as if to prove herself, and then, before either of us could say a thing, she leaned forward and took him into her mouth. I watched in awe as Lisa began to frantically suck off the stranger, and I could no longer contain myself. My hand was on my own cock as he practically fucked her mouth, and her hand was moving just as quickly over her clit.

"Oh god, I'm gonna come," he moaned after just a few minutes, and she squeezed him tightly without stopping. I watched closely as she wrapped her lips around the thick head of his cock, her tongue rolling over him easily. His hand was tight around the base of his shaft, and the entire car instantly smelled like sex as I jerked off faster and faster. Without another warning, he was coming, and Lisa was swallowing all of it as best she could, letting the rest fall onto her bare chest. He groaned, sighed, and then suddenly pulled back as he fell against the seat of his truck.

"Who the hell is driving?" He suddenly asked, looking down at me jerking off in the other seat.

"Drive!" Lisa screamed, her hand still moving as she frantically worked over her clit. I had to force myself to put the car back in gear as the guy stared at us, and she screamed once more. "I said drive uncle Hank!"

Suddenly, and ever so desperately, I wanted the drive to never end.

About The Author

Guy New York is a bestselling erotica author, designer, and degenerate who spends most his time either writing about sex or having it. Sometimes he does both at the same time, much to the chagrin of his partners. With more 35 titles to his name, including two full length novels, three novellas, and numerous short stories, his books have been widely read and often burned. Visit his author site at www.guynewyork.com

Other works by Guy New York:

32 Poems About My Penis

A Cuckold's Diary: The places they Come

A Very Sexy Christmas

A Young and Faithless Wife

All the Groom's Men

Anything for an A

Autumn is Coming

Behind His Back

Boardwalk Affairs (Susanna Part Two)

Camping with the Guys

Caught in the Act

Dirty Bedtime Stories

Disgusting Beautiful Immoral
Everyone Cheats
For the Love of Daddy
Fucking Hilarious
Go Fuck Yourself
Hana
Hotwives and Cheating Girlfriends
Inexcusable Things: A Christmas Story
Love & Kink
MMF
Pill X: The Cure
Pill X: College
Pill X: Spring Break
Private tours: NYC
Punishing Alice
QNY The Complete Stories
QNY: Winter to Spring
Roleplay For Couples
Sex as I Recall
Sex in Cars
Sharing the Wrong Girl
Simply Smut
Susanna's Affairs
Tales of New York
Teacher's New Toy
The Complete Brorotica

The Island on the Edge of Normal
The Ortolan Hunters and Other Disturbing Tales
The Queen's Gentleman
The Summer I Watched My Wife
The Yes Rule
Tracy's Mom
Watching My Wife
Write Till You're Hard

Made in the USA
Middletown, DE
30 April 2022